Just Like
Josh Gibson

written by Angela Johnson

illustrated by Beth Peck

ALADDIN PAPERBACKS

New York London Toronto Sydney

To Art Johnson and all the boys and girls of summer—A. J.

For Brittney and all the other people who modeled for this book. Thank you.
And for my children, Anna Rose and Emma—B. P.

Grandmama says there's nothing like baseball.
The story goes . . .

Josh Gibson once hit a baseball in Pittsburgh
so hard that it didn't come down.

The next day he was playing in Philadelphia
and the ball dropped out of the sky,
right into a fielder's glove.
The umpire pointed at Josh and said,
"You're out yesterday in Pittsburgh!"

Grandmama says her papa showed up
on that same day,
the day she was born,
with a Louisville slugger and a smile.
He said his new baby would make
baseballs fly,
just like Josh Gibson.

So Grandmama's papa threw balls
to his baby girl
in the early morning dew.
Those summer days were like magic
as the balls sailed away,
sailed away,
gone.

But girls in the forties didn't play baseball.
They weren't supposed to take the field with the boys
or have batting dreams.

So even when Grandmama got bigger
she still had to stand outside the fence
and watch her cousin Danny and the Maple Grove All-Stars
batting away.

But every now and again,
when the team was just practicing,
they'd let Grandmama play too.
Then Grandmama would step up to the plate,
hit the ball,
and watch it soar.

Grandmama says
Danny would imagine he was playing with the Dodgers.
But she was always Josh Gibson,
playing for the Grays,
wearing the team colors, and hitting away.

Grandmama says
she would play all day,
with everybody saying
she could do it all,
hit, throw, and fly round the bases.
"But too bad she's a girl . . ."
Too bad she's a girl. . . .

Until . . .
two days, hot days
after the Fourth of July,
Danny hurt his arm sliding into second,
and there were only eight All-Stars.

That afternoon
the team looked to Grandmama—
pink dress with a white bow,
and Danny's baseball shoes.

And Grandmama says
as she went to the plate
she remembered . . .

baseball has always been
early morning dew
and sunlight,

hitting balls with her papa,
and standing behind the fence,
watching the boys play.

The story goes . . .
Grandmama hit the ball a mile that day,
caught anything that was thrown,
and did everything else—
just like Josh Gibson.

As she hands the ball to me
she says, "There's nothing like baseball, baby,
and I couldn't help but love it,
especially that one time I got to hear the cheers,
hear all the cheers,
while stealing home."

Joshua "Josh" Gibson

BORN: December 21, 1911, Buena Vista, Georgia

DIED: January 20, 1947, Pittsburgh, Pennsylvania

BATS: right

THROWS: right

POSITIONS: catcher, outfield

TEAMS: Homestead Grays, Pittsburgh Crawfords

ELECTED TO HALL OF FAME: 1972

Called "the Babe Ruth of the Negro Leagues," the 6'1" Joshua "Josh" Gibson had ball-playing skills that are the stuff of legend. A consummate batter, Gibson hit both for power and average, and is believed to have hit the longest home runs in several big-league parks, including Pittsburgh's Forbes Field, Cincinnati's Crosley Field, and "the House That Ruth Built," Yankee Stadium.[1] In sixty recorded at bats against major-league pitching, he batted a whopping .426. The great Satchel Paige, who was Gibson's teammate on the Pittsburgh Crawfords and who later pitched for the Cleveland Indians, said, "He was the greatest hitter who ever lived."[2]

But Gibson's talent wasn't limited to his performance at the plate. His speed and strong arm made Gibson a force to be reckoned with behind the plate as well, and Hall of Fame pitchers Walter Johnson and Carl Hubbell placed him among baseball's all-time greatest catchers.[3]

Sadly, the major leagues never got a chance to fully welcome Josh Gibson's extraordinary talent. On January 20, 1947, three short months before Jackie Robinson took the field with the Brooklyn Dodgers and ended major-league baseball's fifty-year ban on African-American players, Gibson suffered a stroke and died. He was only thirty-five years old. Years later fellow teammate Judy Johnson would say, "If Josh Gibson had been in the big leagues in his prime, Babe Ruth and Hank Aaron would still be chasing him for the home run record." These are haunting words that remind us of the high cost of arbitrary barriers like race—and gender.

Yet the gender barrier to the "big leagues" still exists. Despite the fact that baseball has fielded several amazing "girl" players, no woman has ever been signed to play for a major-league team. So even though Alta Weiss made enough money pitching exhibition games to put herself through medical school in the early 1900s, and even though seventeen-year-old minor-league pitcher Jackie Mitchell struck out Babe Ruth and Lou Gehrig back-to-back in 1931, the major leagues is still strictly boys only.

There was one young lady during the 1950s that did get to play with the boys though it wasn't in the majors. In 1953 infielder Toni Stone was signed to play the position vacated when slugger Hank Aaron left the Negro Leagues to join the Boston/Milwaukee Braves. Toni was inducted into the Women's Sports Hall of Fame in 1993 and is twice celebrated in Cooperstown, once in the "Women in Baseball" exhibit, and again in the Negro Leagues section. Just like Josh Gibson, she serves as inspiration for all those little ladies with big-league dreams.

[1] Geoffrey C. Ward and Ken Burns, *Baseball: An Illustrated History* (New York: Knopf, 1994).

[2] David Pietrusza, Matthew Silverman, and Michael Gershman, *Baseball: The Biographical Encyclopedia* (New York: Total/Sports Illustrated, 2000).

[3] James A. Riley, *The Biographical Encyclopedia of the Negro Baseball Leagues* (New York: Carroll & Graf, 2002).

ALADDIN PAPERBACKS An imprint of Simon & Schuster Children's Publishing Division 1230 Avenue of the Americas, New York, NY 10020

Text copyright © 2004 by Angela Johnson Illustrations copyright © 2004 by Beth Peck All rights reserved, including the right of reproduction in whole or in part in any form.

ALADDIN PAPERBACKS and colophon are trademarks of Simon & Schuster, Inc. Also available in a Simon & Schuster Books for Young Readers hardcover edition. Designed by Paula Winicur

The text of this book was set in Futura. The illustrations for this book were rendered in pastels on Wallis paper. Manufactured in China First Aladdin Paperbacks edition January 2007

2 4 6 8 10 9 7 5 3 1

The Library of Congress has cataloged the hardcover edition as follows: Johnson, Angela. Just like Josh Gibson / Angela Johnson, Beth Peck p. cm.

Summary: A young girl's grandmother tells her of her love for baseball and the day they let her play in the game even though she was a girl.

ISBN-13: 978-0-689-82628-3 (hc) ISBN-10: 0-689-82628-1 (hc)

[1. Sex role—Fiction. 2. Baseball—Fiction. 3. Grandmothers—Fiction. 4. African Americans—Fiction.] I. Peck, Beth, ill. II. Title. PZ7.J629 Jw2003 [E]—dc21 2001049531

ISBN-13: 978-1-4169-2728-0 (pbk) ISBN-10: 1-4169-2728-X (pbk)